THE BUNNIES' BALL

A Random House PICTUREBACK®

1995

For my son, Eric, with all my love—K.B.

Text copyright © 1994 by Random House, Inc. Illustrations copyright © 1994 by Katy Bratun.
All rights reserved under International and Pan-American Copyright Conventions.
Published in the United States by Random House, Inc., New York, and simultaneously
in Canada by Random House of Canada Limited, Toronto.

Library of Congress Cataloging-in-Publication Data
Ingle, Annie. The Bunnies' Ball / by Annie Ingle ; illustrated by Katy Bratun.
p.   cm. — (A Random House pictureback)
SUMMARY: A rhyming look behind the scenes at all the magical preparations of the
forest animals for the night that the bunnies dance.   ISBN 0-679-83503-2 (pbk.)
[1. Animals—Fiction.   2. Rabbits—Fiction.   3. Balls (Parties)—Fiction.   4. Stories in rhyme.]
I. Bratun, Katy, ill.   II. Title.   PZ8.3.I62Bu   1994   [E]—dc20   93-8536

Manufactured in the United States of America   10 9 8 7 6 5 4 3

THE BUNNIES' BALL

by **ANNIE INGLE**

illustrated by
KATY BRATUN

Random House New York

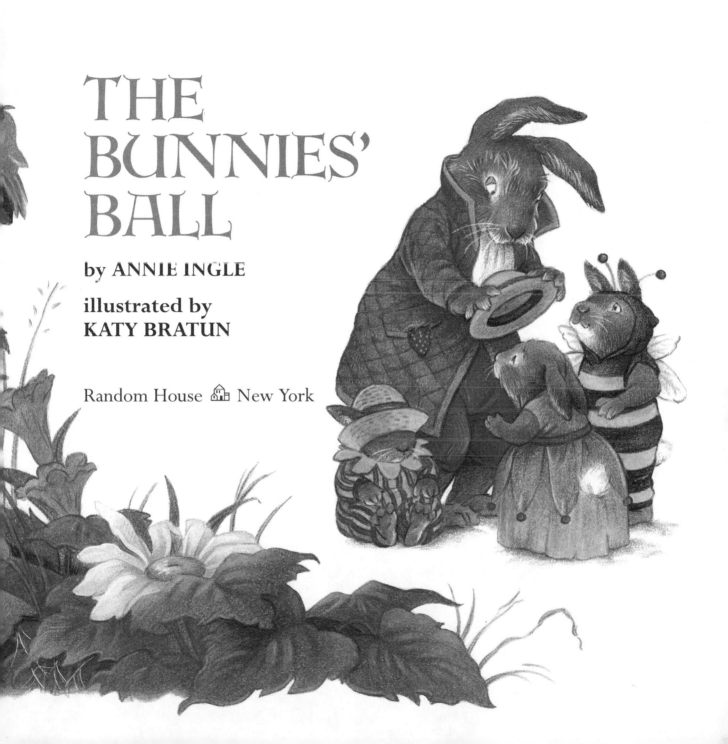

When the moon is full

and the air is sweet

and the crickets

begin to thrum…

and fireflies flicker

and raccoons bicker

and the bullfrog

beats soft his drum…

slip on your sweater
and sneak to the woods
and crouch in the dark
on your knees.

You might just see
a wondrous sight
that only the
lucky ones see.

It's the Bunnies' Ball!
A splendid dance,
and all good bunnies
are there—

cottontail, jackrabbit,
lop-ear,
and, of course,
the Belgian hare.

Down in the warrens,
little ones
sing and
bounce upon their beds,
while mothers adorn
their ears with flowers
and dads set
their hats
on their heads.

Up in the clearing,
the busy squirrels sweep
the dance floor
clean and clear.

And fireflies nestle
in bluebell shades
as party time
slowly draws near.

The gray moths drape
the twigs and branches
with chains of
fragrant flowers.

And more moths spray
cool water on blooms
to keep them
fresh for hours.

And chipmunks fix
a sumptuous feast
of dew and
dandelion punch,
of crackers smeared
with carrot cream,
of watercress quiche
to munch.
There are tortes and tarts
and turnip tops and ices to
last the night.
For chipmunks know
it is their job
to get each
detail right.

The musicians come
a little late—
but better late
than never.
For far and wide
these minstrels are known
as the greatest
dance band ever.

Three tree frogs,
a cricket quartet,
a beaver who
plays his tail.
Two wild dogs,
a shrill katydid,
and a soulful
nightingale.

The band is set,
the instruments tuned,
there falls
a sudden hush,
as Old Groundhog
makes his rounds
with snow-white
gloves and brush.

The trumpets blare,
and doors swing wide.
The bunnies
two by two
emerge in moonlight,
blinking, preening,
sashaying
into view.

O elegant bunnies!
They waltz
and whirl
in finery and pomp.

Then the band
picks up the beat
and the bunnies
start to stomp.
They romp, they kick,
they rock, they roll,
they shake loose leaves
from the trees.
In all your life
you've never seen
such revelers
as these!

So now you've
seen the
wondrous sight
that only the lucky
ones see.
It's time to come
out of the bushes
and dust off
both your knees.

Go on home,
you've had enough,
you've surely
had your fill

of berry tarts
and carrot cream
and tasty treats,
until…

the moon is full
and the air is sweet
and the crickets
begin to thrum
and fireflies flicker
and raccoons bicker
and the bullfrog
beats soft his drum.